Flash Harriet
and the Mystery of the Fiendish Footprints

D1393551

Written by Karen Wallace

Illustrated by Andy Rowland

 Collins

1 Two peculiar people

Flash Harriet was sitting in her tree house, trying not to listen to the sound of her father banging on his piano. BOING! BANG! BOING! It was Norman Brilliant's most famous noise and he liked to play it every day.

SMASH! SMASH! SMASH! Flash Harriet's mother, Sequin Cynthia, was standing on top of the roof spinning plates. It was her favourite acrobatic act, but right now it wasn't going very well.

Flash Harriet was reading a book called *Daring Detectives*. Her Uncle Proudlock had written it and he was the best detective in the business.

SMASH! BANG! Flash Harriet put down her book. Even though she was a good detective like her uncle, she still needed peace and quiet so that she could concentrate.

Across the room, Gus, her pet tarantula, rolled his eyes. Gus had been Uncle Proudlock's idea. "Best guard dog you can find," he'd said. And he was right, even though Flash Harriet knew that Gus was really as sweet as a kitten.

"I'm going to the park to read my book,"
said Flash Harriet to Gus as she reached for
the fireman's pole she used for quick exits.
"Look after the place, okay?"

Gus was about to waggle his legs in reply when
there was a sharp knock at the door.

KNOCK!
KNOCK!

Flash Harriet quickly returned to her desk. A woman with a face like a weasel strode into the room. She was wearing lime-green Wellington boots decorated with vegetable stickers.

"I'm Daphne Beane," she said, holding out her hand. "Daphne Beane, the Gardening Queen. I haven't got any time to waste, so you'd better stop what you're doing and listen!"

Flash Harriet decided she didn't like the look of Daphne Beane. "How can I help you?" she asked.

"It's about *dear* Marmaduke Mildew," said Daphne Beane. "Frankie Leather and Muriel Grunt want to have him thrown out of the Giant Vegetable Competition, because he's so crazy about winning. But as I'm his friend, I've come to warn you."

"Warn me about what?" asked Flash Harriet, coldly.

Daphne Beane narrowed her eyes, "Warn you that the competition will be ruined unless you do something about Marmaduke. He's gone loopy."

"I beg your pardon?"

"Loopy. Nuts. Crazy!" snapped Daphne Beane. "You're the detective! You find out!" Then she smirked at Flash Harriet. "But if you want a tip from me, watch out for Frankie. He just *hates* poor Marmaduke."

Then Daphne left, slamming the door behind her.

Flash Harriet looked at Gus, who was lying on his back, waggling his legs in the air. It was his way of telling her that something suspicious was going on! And he was right.

Five minutes later, there was a squelching noise and a man as soggy as a wet teddy bear struggled up the fireman's pole.

"My name is Marmaduke Mildew," he said, sounding as if he was trying hard not to burst into tears. "And I really need your help."

Flash Harriet felt sorry for Marmaduke immediately, despite what Daphne Beane had said about him. He had droopy, brown eyes and a lump of mud on his head that he didn't seem to notice. "Tell me everything," she said. "I'll help you if I can."

So Marmaduke explained about the Giant Vegetable Competition. It was the 100th anniversary and it was going to be the biggest vegetable competition the town had ever put on.

There were four competitors: himself with his giant leeks, Daphne Beane with her huge pumpkins, Muriel Grunt with her gigantic carrots and Frankie Leather with his enormous onions.

"Everyone knows that it all depends on
the vegetables and the best gardener will win,"
cried Marmaduke, clearly upset, "but last night
a monster trampled all over the garden.
Only two days before the competition!"

"What kind of monster?" asked Flash Harriet.

"I don't know," replied Marmaduke, "but it's got feet
like an elephant and they're all blaming me!"

Flash Harriet frowned. "Why?"

"Because I feed the elephants at the zoo," replied
Marmaduke. He buried his head in his hands and
the lump of mud fell on the floor. "They've even
banned me from the vegetable garden, so now I
can't look after my leeks."

"Just tell me how to get to the garden and I'll look
after your leeks," said Flash Harriet, firmly.
"And don't worry about that monster.
I'm on the case!"

2 Monster footprints

Ten minutes later, armed with a bottle of "Jumbo Juice" for Marmaduke Mildew's giant leeks, Flash Harriet set off for the vegetable garden on her motor-powered tricycle.

Suddenly, a shiny gold Ferrari with a silver onion on the bonnet roared past her. The driver had a sharp, hard face and a diamond ring with an "F" on it sparkled on his little finger.

I wonder if that's Frankie Leather, thought Flash Harriet. She didn't like the look of him one bit. Then she saw the person sitting beside him and almost fell off her trike.

It was Daphne Beane and there was a nasty smile on her face.

Something fishy was going on!

Flash Harriet followed Marmaduke's instructions for getting to the garden, and, before long, she spotted a heavy iron door. She turned three different keys in three different locks. It was like going into a high-security bank vault.

As she opened the door, a woman jumped out at her wearing a yellow boiler suit. It had MURIEL GRUNT – CRANE DRIVER on it.

"Get out!" she yelled. "You're trespassing!"

"I want to ask some questions about your vegetables," replied Flash Harriet in a firm voice. To her astonishment, Muriel threw herself on the ground and rolled about in the mud, waving her arms and legs about.

"It's not fair! I always get left out," she howled. "I want to win, but that monster's *ruining* my carrots!"

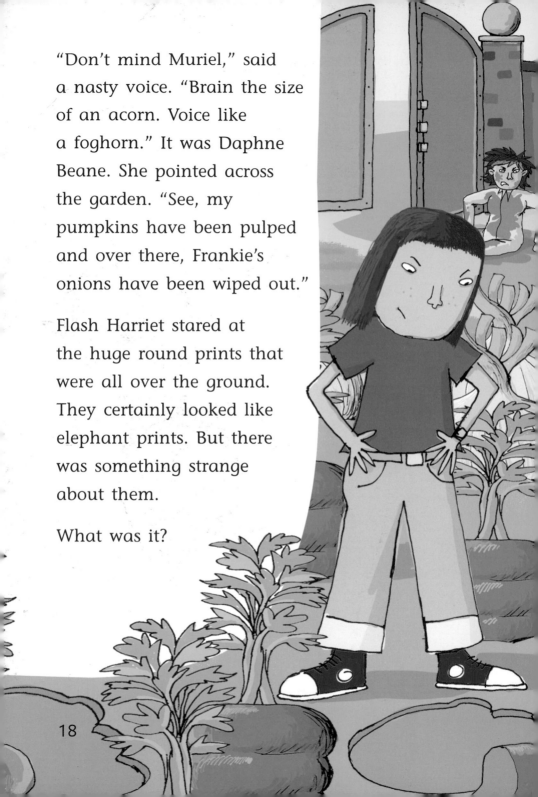

"Don't mind Muriel," said a nasty voice. "Brain the size of an acorn. Voice like a foghorn." It was Daphne Beane. She pointed across the garden. "See, my pumpkins have been pulped and over there, Frankie's onions have been wiped out."

Flash Harriet stared at the huge round prints that were all over the ground. They certainly looked like elephant prints. But there was something strange about them.

What was it?

Then she realised that if the prints *had* been made by an elephant, it was a very *tidy* elephant. The big round holes were in neat lines and part of each vegetable patch had been left untouched, which meant that all the competitors still had a chance to win!

There was a screech of brakes. A gold Ferrari skidded to a halt and the man with the sharp face jumped out.

"Such a shame about Marmaduke," sneered Frankie Leather without bothering to introduce himself. "He's in terrible trouble, you know. These footprints belong to an elephant." Frankie smiled a smile like an alligator's. "Just like the ones he looks after at the zoo. If you ask me, he'll be back tonight to smash the rest of our vegetables!"

Flash Harriet thought hard. It looked as if Frankie was right about the footprints, but why was he trying so hard to blame Marmaduke? And why had Daphne Beane told her to watch out for Frankie and then gone driving around with him in his car?

There was one way to find out. Flash got out her phone and texted her Uncle Proudlock in Scotland.

3 Follow your hunch

The next day, a pigeon wearing a tartan scarf flopped through the window on to Flash Harriet's desk.

There was a message tied to its leg. It said: *Follow your hunch. Uncle P.*

Flash Harriet stared at the tiny piece of paper. Uncle Proudlock was telling her to trust her own judgment. But the problem was she didn't *have* a hunch! Any of the competitors could be cheating.

An open newspaper on her desk caught her eye. The headline said: *"Mayor's Vital Vegetable Quest!"*

Flash Harriet read on. The Mayor was going to judge the Giant Vegetable Competition the next day and the prize was a very special secret.

Flash Harriet felt the hairs on the back of her neck prickle. Maybe it was time to pay the Mayor a visit!

An hour later, Flash Harriet was standing in the Mayor's enormous office. "This competition is VITAL!" he squawked, hopping from foot to foot.

Flash Harriet looked at Gus and rolled her eyes. "Please, Mr Mayor," she said firmly, "just tell me everything."

The Mayor took a deep breath. "As a special 100th anniversary prize," he said, pausing at every word, "whoever wins the competition will get to keep the vegetable garden *forever*." He looked worried. "All three competitors have promised to keep growing vegetables there, but I must be *sure* that the winner's telling the truth. Otherwise, the town will lose its vegetable garden – and we really need those vegetables for our school dinners!"

"Surely, you mean *four* competitors," said Flash Harriet in a puzzled voice.

The Mayor pulled a letter out of his pocket. "Marmaduke Mildew has ridden an elephant over the garden and almost destroyed everyone's vegetables." The Mayor paused. "I'm throwing him out of the competition for cheating."

"He's *not* a cheat!" cried Flash Harriet. "I'm sure he's not. Besides, his leeks were trampled on, too!" Flash fixed the Mayor with a fierce stare. "Who sent you that letter?"

"There was no name on the bottom," replied the Mayor, as if it didn't matter. "Anyway, that still doesn't explain the elephant. Marmaduke Mildew is the only one who knows how to ride one!"

"He only feeds them," insisted Flash Harriet. As she spoke, she thought of Daphne Beane and Frankie Leather in the Ferrari together and Muriel Grunt yelling, "It's not fair! I always get left out."

Left out of what?

Flash Harriet made up her mind. It was time for action!

"Meet me at the vegetable garden tonight and bring along some floodlights," she said to the Mayor. "I'll show you your so-called elephant!"

4 Caught in the lights

Flash Harriet crouched amongst the vegetables in the darkness. Even though Gus was in his cage beside her, she had never felt so nervous in all her life. What if she was wrong?

She had no proof that Marmaduke wasn't the cheat, only a strong feeling in the pit of her stomach and her Uncle Proudlock's message: *Follow your hunch.* Just then, the Mayor crawled across the wet grass towards her.

"Did you bring the floodlights?" whispered
Flash Harriet.

The Mayor nodded and handed over the remote
control. "You'd better be right about this,"
he muttered crossly. "My trousers are *ruined*!"

They heard the sound of a car engine at the gate.

"Shh!" said Flash Harriet. "Someone's coming!"

31

Flash Harriet and the Mayor watched in stunned silence as Daphne Beane and Frankie Leather climbed out of the Ferrari, pulled plastic wastepaper baskets in the shape of an elephant's foot over their boots and began stomping all over the ground.

"Oi," growled Frankie, "mind my onions! I won't have any left for the competition!"

"You stay off my pumpkins, then," snarled Daphne.

"Who cares about your pumpkins?" sneered Frankie. "We agreed. I win the competition and you get my Ferrari. And then I'm going to turn the garden into a multi-storey car park."

"Rubbish!" screeched Daphne. "I got Muriel to play along with us. I told that stupid detective that Marmaduke had gone crazy. So *I* win. You can keep your Ferrari because I'm building a Keep Fit Centre." She shoved her face into his. "Then I'll knock you out with one big *punch*!"

"Sorry, dumb brain," Frankie yelled back nastily, "you've got it wrong." He smashed a pumpkin as big as a tent. "It was *my* idea to write to that dope of a Mayor and tell him that Marmaduke was a cheat!" Flash Harriet heard an angry spluttering noise beside her.

"Shh!" she whispered to the Mayor. "It's not over yet."

Sure enough, the next moment Muriel Grunt sailed over the garden wall on an enormous pogo stick! A huge rubber elephant's foot was stuck to the end. Even Flash Harriet gasped.

"Cheats!" Muriel screamed at Frankie and Daphne. "You were going to crush all my carrots! You were going to leave me out and win the competition for yourselves!"

She landed right in the middle of Frankie's onions. "Well – I'll – show – you – both!"

Muriel bounced over to smash the rest of Daphne's pumpkins.

"I've got my own plans!" Muriel shrieked. "*I'm* going to win the competition and I'm building a Mud Wrestling Club! *Crane drivers only.*"

Flash Harriet watched in horror as Muriel turned in mid-air and headed towards Marmaduke Mildew's leeks.

There was only one thing to do.

She switched on the floodlights.

5   A very special favour

"Disgusting! Disgraceful!" bellowed the Mayor at the three cheats, who stood frozen like statues in the bright white light. "I'm ashamed to be standing in the same garden as you, you vegetable vandals!"

Frankie burst into tears and Muriel threw herself on the ground and began to howl. But Daphne saw her chance.

"If *I* can't win, *nobody* wins!" Daphne yelled at the top of her voice, as she ran towards the last row of Marmaduke Mildew's leeks.

Flash Harriet flicked open the catch of Gus's travelling cage. "Quick, Gus!" she shouted. "Stop her!"

Speedier than a shooting star, Gus soared through
the air and landed like a furry octopus on top of
Daphne's head.

Daphne opened her mouth to yell, but Gus clamped
a hairy leg over her front teeth and she fell to
the ground with a wet *thump*.

"My leeks!" cried a squeaky voice. "I must see my leeks!"

Someone who looked like a soggy teddy bear ran up the path towards the row of tall green leaves. "My darlings! My lovelies!" sniffled Marmaduke Mildew. "Are you all right?"

Flash Harriet and the Mayor stared in astonishment as Marmaduke wrapped his arms around his leeks.

The Mayor coughed in an embarrassed sort of way.
"Uh, sorry to interrupt you, Mildew," he muttered.

Marmaduke nearly jumped out of his skin.
"Mr Mayor!" he cried. "I didn't see you!"
He grabbed the Mayor's hand in his muddy
one. "How can I thank you for saving my leeks?"

"Don't thank me," replied the Mayor, trying hard to pull his hand free. "It was Flash Harriet. She believed you were innocent and she brought me here to prove it."

Marmaduke looked at them in amazement. "But how? I don't understand!"

"It's quite simple," said Flash Harriet. "There was something fishy about those elephant prints. They were too tidy – and they were all *left feet*! Like Uncle Proudlock told me, I followed a hunch. I just knew you were the one who really loved the garden."

"Congratulations, Marmaduke," said the Mayor. "It looks as if this vegetable garden is yours!"

"Mine?" gasped Marmaduke Mildew. "You mean ..."

"Yes!" cried the Mayor excitedly. "You're going to win the Giant Vegetable Competition." He pointed to the remaining row of leeks gleaming like leafy ivory towers in the floodlights. "I've never seen such huge, beautiful leeks in all of my life."

Marmaduke turned to Flash Harriet. "May I ask you a favour?" he said shyly.

"Of course!"

"May I name the garden after you?"
Marmaduke Mildew looked around at the rows of
crushed vegetables. "When I've done the digging
and made it look lovely again, of course."

"I'd be honoured," replied Flash Harriet.
"I've never had a vegetable garden named after
me." She turned and winked at the Mayor.
"And as for doing the digging, I know just
the people for the job!"

As the three cheats pulled furious faces,
the Mayor burst out laughing. "Flash Harriet!"
he cried, "You're a genius! And the most brilliant
detective, ever!"

45

Flash Harriet solves the case

Here are the clues:

1 Daphne says she isn't Frankie's friend, then rides with him in the car.

2 Muriel wails that Daphne and Frankie are always leaving her out.

3 The elephant tracks are all left feet and are too tidy.

4 Some of each competitor's vegetables are left, so anyone could still win the competition.

5 The competition winner will get the garden for ever, to use as they like.

6 The Mayor gets a letter accusing Marmaduke because he works with elephants.

7 All the competitors want to win, but Marmaduke seems to love his vegetables the most.

:paw: Ideas for guided reading :paw:

Getting started

This book can be read over two or more guided reading sessions.

- Read the title and blurb and look at the picture on the front cover together. Discuss what is unusual about Harriet, e.g. *she is a detective, has a pet tarantula*, and what characteristics she might have.

- Read pp2–5 to the children. Check that children understand what a detective is and what they do, use a dictionary. Ask children to predict what is going to happen in the story based on their reading of the blurb and the information so far.

Reading and responding

- Model how to collect information and make notes from reading about Flash Harriet using pp2–5 (*father is a musician, mother is an acrobat, Harriet is an aspiring detective, needs peace and quiet etc.*).

- Ask children to step into the role of detective, and collect as much information as they can about the characters that are mentioned in pp6–9: Daphne Bean, Marmaduke Mildew, Frankie Leather, Muriel Grunt.

- Ask children to share their ideas about the characters who will be involved in the mystery. Discuss what they understand about the mystery and what they think will happen next.